W9-BUC-910

Lily and the Paper Man

by Rebecca Upjohn
illustrated by Renné Benoit

Second Story Press

"Shall we take the bus home today?" Lily's mother asks.

Lily peers from under her umbrella. "Let's walk. I *like* the rain." She takes her mother's hand to cross the street. Her mother goes around the puddles. Lily skips through them.

"Good-bye, Frank," she calls to the crossing guard.

Frank holds up his bright red STOP sign for her. "Good-bye, Lily. See you tomorrow."

R0447558739

*D*own the street they go. Lily hops on one foot past the window of Mrs. Chan's store. She waves at Mrs. Chan, who smiles and waves back. They are almost home.

"Look, Mama. I can walk backwards the rest of the way."

"Be careful, Lily," her mother cries.

Lily backs into something. She spins around.

"A dollar for the paper," growls a tall man in a raggedy coat. His hair sticks up higgledy-piggledy all over his head. He thrusts a thin newspaper toward Lily's mother. Lily hides, clutching her mother's coat as she peeks out.

Her mother gives the man a dollar and takes the paper. "Thank you," she says.

The man nods and then stares at Lily. The rain runs off his bumpy nose and down into his beard. Lily can hear his wheezy breathing. She clings to her mother, looking back all the way to their apartment door.

The next day after school, Lily says, "I want to take the bus home, Mama."

"Are you sure?"

Lily looks at her feet and nods, so they get in line and board the bus. She sees Frank out the window and waves, but he doesn't see her. They whiz past Mrs. Chan's too fast for Lily to see her friendly face. When they drive past the Paper Man, Lily ducks down in her seat. He doesn't see her! Her mother rings the bell.

Lily runs from the bus to the lobby door. "Hurry, hurry, Mama!" She pushes against the handle.

"Is something wrong, Lily?"

Lily shakes her head and looks down the street. The Paper Man is heading their way. Lily feels his eyes on her. She shoves the door and it clicks shut. They are safe now.

All that week Lily and her mother take the bus. And all the next week. And every day after that. Until the first snow falls.

Lily has fleecy new mitts and toasty new boots. She tries to catch snowflakes on her tongue.

"Try it, Mama," she says. She tugs on her mother's hand.

"Don't you want to take the bus, Lily?"

Lily shakes her head. "I *like* the snow. Good-bye, Frank." They cross the street. Snow flies around them in a bright flurry.

"Let's see if Mrs. Chan is selling hot cocoa yet," Lily's mother says. Lily claps her mittens together and runs on ahead.

Lily closes her eyes and listens to the squeak and crunch of her boots in the snow. Her mother follows her.

"A dollar for the paper..."

*L*ily's eyes fly open. The Paper Man holds out a newspaper with a shaking hand. Lily wants to run away, but she stands still. She sees a thin shirt through the holes in his coat and bare feet through the holes in his boots. Lily shivers.

Lily's mother gives the man a dollar, then she tucks the paper into her purse. "Thank you," she says.

"Have a good day," says the Paper Man. Lily is not sure, but she thinks he winks at her.

*L*ily forgets to press the numbers that unlock the lobby door. She forgets to push the UP button on the elevator. She is thinking.

"Lily, is something wrong?"

"The Paper Man isn't wearing socks, Mama. Why? It's cold out."

Lily's mother looks serious. "I guess he doesn't have any," she says. "We're very lucky to have warm clothes and a place to live."

Lily is quiet after that and holds her mother's hand all the way to their apartment.

On Saturday Lily goes out with her father to buy milk at Mrs. Chan's. The Paper Man is on the corner. He has no hat and his ears are red from the cold. Lily's father stops to buy a paper.

"Thank you," says the Paper Man. Then, "Morning, missy." He smiles a wobbly smile.

Inside the store Lily has the dollar her father gave her for a treat, but she can't decide what to buy.

"Save it until you find something special," suggests Mrs. Chan.

*L*ily walks home hand in hand with her father. She feels the coins in her mitten press against her palm. They come to the corner. There he is again. The Paper Man's shoulders are hunched. His arms are folded and Lily sees him shuffling from one cold foot to the other. He doesn't even notice her this time.

That night in bed, Lily snuggles down under her favorite quilt. She holds her doll, Steffie, close.

"We are warm, and we have enough socks. But the Paper Man is cold. What can we do, Steffie?" Lily thinks and thinks until her question fades into sleep.

In the morning, Lily slips out of bed and, hugging Steffie, whispers, "I know what to do!"

The next day after school, Lily and her mother stop to talk to Frank. Then they go to Mrs. Chan's store. Then they visit the caretaker in their building. All week Lily works on her idea. She and her father go to this place and that, fetching and carrying until, at last, she is ready. Under her quilt that night, Lily has trouble falling asleep.

Early, early, Lily wakes up. She and Steffie hurry into her parents' room. "It's time to get *up*," she says.

"Go back to bed, Lily, it's too early," mumbles her father.

"It's Saturday," her mother adds.

"The wind is blowing and the snow is falling," says Lily. "The Paper Man is cold. Please come *now*."

Lily's mother sits up in bed. Her father turns on the light. They look at each other and they get out of bed. They get dressed, pick up a big, big bag, and down they go.

Outside, the wind is blowing from the North Pole. The Paper Man is on the corner. Lily feels her heart thumping, but she takes the bag from her father and drags it over the snow, right up to the Paper Man's feet.

"Morning, missy," he says.

"My name is Lily." She holds out her hand.

The Paper Man shakes it. "My name is Ray. That's a whole lot of garbage you have there."

Lily smiles. "It's not garbage. It's a present. For you." She notices his nose is red from the wind. She rubs her own cold nose. "Open it," she says.

The Paper Man peeks inside the bag and lifts out a sweater. Lily looks back at her father. Ray pulls the sweater on over his coat. He reaches in again, and out comes a thick pair of socks. He sits down and puts them on. Now Lily can see orange flowers through the holes in Ray's boots. She winks at her mother.

Next the Paper Man puts on a stripy hat with earflaps. Lily claps her hands. He looks just like Frank. Then he pulls on the new gloves and scarf that Mrs. Chan gave her for her special dollar. Ray keeps reaching in and putting on more, until he is so puffy he can barely bend.

From the very bottom he pulls out Lily's quilt, the one her granny made her for being born.

The Paper Man holds it up and looks at the stars and elephants and turtles. Lily tries to smile, but it is her very favorite quilt. The Paper Man wraps it around himself.

"Thank you, Lily," he says softly.

"Now you are warm," she says, past the lump in her throat.

"I'm warmer than I've been for a long, long time." His eyes sparkle. He smiles the biggest smile Lily has ever seen. Suddenly, she can smile again too.

"The Paper Man is warm," says Lily, as she and her parents walk home. In the lobby, Lily presses her nose against the frosty window and looks out.

The Paper Man waves at her. He is still smiling. Happily, Lily waves back.

LIBRARY AND ARCHIVES CANADA CATALOGUING IN PUBLICATION

Upjohn, Rebecca, 1962–
Lily and the paper man / by Rebecca Upjohn ;
illustrated by Renné Benoit.

ISBN 978-1-897187-19-7

I. Benoit, Renné II. Title.
PS8641.P386L54 2007 jC813'.6 C2007-902305-3

Text copyright © 2007 by Rebecca Upjohn Snyder
Illustrations copyright © 2007 by Renné Benoit
Designed by Melissa Kaita
Rebecca Upjohn's photo © Aarin MacKay
Visit Rebecca Upjohn's website at www.rebeccaupjohn.com

Second Story Press gratefully acknowledges the support
of the Ontario Arts Council and the Canada Council for
the Arts for our publishing program. We acknowledge the
financial support of the Government of Canada through
the Book Publishing Industry Development Program.

ONTARIO ARTS COUNCIL
CONSEIL DES ARTS DE L'ONTARIO

Canada Council   Conseil des Arts
for the Arts   du Canada

Published by
SECOND STORY PRESS
20 Maud Street, Suite 401
Toronto, Ontario, Canada

For Don, Harris and
Emmett who keep me
from the cold
— R.U.

For my Dad
— R.B.

Thank you to Susan M.
Chapman and Jillian Pearson
for helping to hone Lily's story.
— R.U.